The Goosehill Gang
and the
C. B. Convoy Caper

by Mary Blount Christian
illustrated by Betty Wind

Now there are varieties of gifts, but the same
Spirit; and there are varieties of service, but
the same Lord.
1 Corinthians 12:4-5 RSV

Publishing House
St. Louis

To Devin, my son and technical advisor

Concordia Publishing House, St. Louis, Missouri
Copyright © 1977 Concordia Publishing House
Manufactured in the United States of America

Library of Congress Cataloging in Publication Data
Christian, Mary Blount
    The Goosehill Gang and the C.B. Convoy caper
    SUMMARY: Using the C.B. radios, the Goosehill Gang uncovers a ring of bicycle
thieves in their neighborhood.
[1. Mystery and detective stories. 2. Citizens band radio—fiction] I. Wind, Betty
II. Title.
PZ 7.C4528Gk   (Fic)   77-5766
ISBN 0-570-07352-9

Marcus bent over the pile of metal and plastic, studying it. At last he twisted two wires together and grinned with satisfaction. "There!" he said.

Beth squatted beside him. "What are you doing with all this junk?"

Marcus shoved his glasses back on his nose. "Junk? I'll show you junk!" He handed her one of the walkie-talkies. "Take this around the corner of the house. And when you get there, push this button," he instructed her.

Beth did as Marcus said. The box crackled with static. "Breaker one," a voice said. It was Marcus. "This is Wild Goose. Got your ears on?"

"Huh?" Beth said. "Marcus?"

He came around the corner. "I bought these at a garage sale down the street for 50 cents because they were broken. The other one belongs to Ronny."

"Who?"

"You know, the teenager next door to me. His bike was stolen and he needed one for his work. I lent him mine. These are—how do you say it— col-lateral."

Beth's eyes brightened. "You mean if you don't get your bike back you can keep these walkie-talkies?"

Marcus frowned at her. "These may be fun, but they don't have wheels. I miss my bike, but Ronny needed it, so I'll manage until he finds his, or gets another one."

Tubby, Don, and Pete parked their bikes by Beth's. They joined the other two members of the Goosehill Gang. "What's up?" asked Don. "Why the early call?"

"Look!" Beth squealed. "Isn't this clever? Marcus fixed these. Now we can be C.B.ers like the grownups."

Marcus shrugged. "Yeah, but I only have three."

Tubby's face brightened. "Hey! I still have a pair put away. I got them from Aunt Harriet for Christmas when I was a little kid. Good ol' Aunt Harriet."

"Get them," Beth suggested. "And we'll all meet at the tree house. We can play C.B. convoy."

Later on at the tree house the gang chattered excitedly. Marcus passed out papers with some of

the C.B. code language. "Now we can do it just like the truckers," he said.

"We have to make up names, I mean *handles,*" Don said.

"All the handles should have something to do with the Goosehill Gang," Marcus suggested. "Mine's Wild Goose."

Don sighed. "Well, after our last baseball game, I guess mine should be Goose Egg!"

Pete laughed. "I guess since I want to be a writer someday, I'll be Goose Quill, like the pens old-time writers used. What about you, Tubby?"

Tubby patted his stomach and grinned. "Me? I'm going to be Stuffed Goose!"

Beth giggled. She spread her arms like wings. "My favorite stories are still the old ones, so mine will be Mother Goose!"

Each member picked up a walkie-talkie, scrambled down the ladder, and scooted in opposite directions. "Breaker one! Mother Goose to Goose Egg," called Beth. "Are you listening? I mean, got your ears on?"

Don snickered and searched his page of codes. "You got the Goose Egg, here, wall to wall and 10 feet tall."

"Breaker to the Stuffed Goose. What's your ten twenty?" Marcus' voice interrupted. There was no answer. "Stuffed Goose, come in. Tubby! Have you got peanut butter in your ears?"

"Mother Goose to Wild Goose," Beth said laughing. "I think Stuffed Goose took a seven at the bean store."

"Bean store?" Pete interrupted. "Come back with that copy again."

"Where the food is," Beth translated. "I think the Goose is getting stuffed again."

There was a sudden break, "Stuffed Goose to all the Geese. Eyeball at the tree house." Through the static Tubby's voice sounded frantic. "And Geese," he added. "Put the hammer down."

They all knew Tubby meant for them to hurry. Each answered "ten four," for yes. Within minutes they were back at the tree house.

"What's up?" Beth asked.

"Looks like that bike bandit that's been ripping off the other neighborhoods is here now," Tubby moaned. "My brand-new ten speed was in front of my house. I went in to get an apple and when I came out it was gone. I wasn't gone more than a minute."

"Did you lock your bike?" questioned Don.

"No, not right in front of my house." Tubby looked miserable.

"I haven't even had time to register the serial number with the police."

Don thought for a moment. "Let's fan out and call in every few minutes. If you see anything suspicious, call in," he said. "Don't try to handle it alone," he warned.

"That sounds great," said Pete. He gave Tubby
a sympathetic pat on the shoulder. "Hey, good
buddy, don't worry. We'll find your wheels." He
scrambled down the ladder of the tree house, and
the others followed. They moved out slowly in
opposite directions, Marcus and Tubby on foot and
the others on their bikes.

"Breaker one for the Stuffed Goose. Give me a
shout," Marcus called.

"You've got the Stuffed Goose," Tubby
answered. "My ten twenty is Elm and Spruce."

Beth reported she was at Main and Walker.
Don was further down Main. Marcus was on the
bike trail near Pine, and Pete was scouting on
Maple. Marcus spoke. "Breaker for the Geese. This
is Wild Goose. Eyeball at Elm and Oak. And
hurry!"

When they reached him, Marcus was with his neighbor, Ronny. Ronny was sitting with his head in his hands. He hardly spoke when Marcus introduced him to the gang. "Marcus' bike was stolen right out from under me," Ronny told them. "You must think I'm pretty dumb to get TWO bikes stolen right under my nose."

"No we don't. It could happen to anybody," Tubby said, thinking about his own bike.

"I'm still paying for my own bike. And now this!" Ronny shook his head sadly.

"That makes three bikes stolen in Goosehill in less than 24 hours," Don said. "I bet there's more than one thief. They are probably working together to be able to get rid of the bikes so fast."

Ronny explained how he was delivering a package for Bell's Pharmacy when the bike was stolen. "I looked just in time to see a boy in brown jeans and a faded army jacket jump on Marcus' bike and speed away." Ronny shrugged apologetically. "I didn't get a good look at his face. I have to be the dumbest jerk in Goosehill."

Beth blinked. "No, Ronny! I'm afraid you're only a close second." She slapped her forehead. "I saw a boy in a faded army jacket. I should've known that was Marcus' bike. I just wasn't thinking."

"You saw him?" Don asked.

Beth nodded. "I got a good look at his face, too. His pants leg got tangled in the bike chain and he had to stop for a minute. I'd recognize him again, I know!"

"Where was that?" Pete asked.

"At the corner of Walker and Elm. He was crossing Elm going East. I rode right past him."

Don scratched his chin thoughtfully. "That's strange. I was at Main and Walker within seconds and I didn't see him there."

Beth picked up a stick and drew in the dirt. "Tubby and Marcus were here," she said, pointing to where two lines crossed.

"I get it, Beth," Pete said. "We'll make a map and see where we were and where the suspect was seen. By figuring out where we were, we can pinpoint where he might have gone."

"Hey!" Ronny bragged. "That's pretty smart! I never would've thought of that, and I'm a whole lot older!"

Beth continued to draw in the dirt. She marked

where each member was when she spotted the boy on Marcus' bike. "That does it!" Don said. "He must've gone into a building on Walker. I'd guess somewhere between Elm and Pine."

"What kind of buildings are on Walker?" Marcus asked. "All of you have lived here longer than I have."

"Mostly small businesses," said Tubby. "There's a Burger Palace on Pine, and Pizza Parlor on Walker, and a . . ."

"Sure, Tubby," Don interrupted. "We know where all the restaurants are, but I think we're looking for something different." Tubby blushed.

"There's a drug store on Elm, and a car wash on Walker," Pete added.

Marcus slammed his fist in his palm. "I've got an idea." He turned to Ronny. "You're very good at drawing, aren't you? Can you draw what Beth describes to you?"

"Well, before I quit school last year my teacher used to brag about my pictures." He laughed. "It's all she ever did brag about, come to think of it. I didn't do very well in school. But me draw? I haven't drawn a lick since I dropped out. Not even as a hobby!"

Marcus ignored him. "We'll need a pencil and some paper," he said. Don brought them down from the tree house. The gang huddled together while Beth described the thief to Ronny. She made faces as she tried to remember every detail. Ronny's pencil flicked as Beth described the boy.

"No," she corrected. "The eyes are closer together. That's it. Now, thicker eyebrows. Right! That's him. That's really him!" she shouted.

"Aw," Ronny apologized. "I bet it doesn't look like him. I probably goofed it up. I usually do."

The gang hurried to the library and made a photo copy of the picture for each of them. They locked their remaining bikes around a telephone pole and walked.

Pete rubbed his legs. "Tubby, if you ride double with me again, you'll have to pedal," he said puffing.

They fanned out again in the area where Beth had seen the boy. They showed the picture to shop keepers on all the streets, but no one recognized the thief from the picture. "It's probably because I didn't draw the picture very well," Ronny told Marcus as they turned toward the car wash on Walker.

18

"It's fine, Ronny. Really it is." Marcus pushed open the door to the car wash office. "This one must be it," Marcus said. "The other door says 'No Admittance.'"

"We ain't hiring no help," the big man at the desk said, hardly looking up. "And if we was, it wouldn't be no kids."

Marcus pulled his shoulders back and tried to look taller. "We're not here for a job, Sir." He shoved the picture toward the man. "Have you seen anyone who looks like this around here?"

The man stared at the picture. His mouth slowly opened. He swallowed hard. "No! What are you, anyway? The midget CIA? I ain't never seen nobody looking like this. I'm busy."

Marcus got the picture and the boys thanked the man and left. Marcus grabbed Ronny's sleeve and pulled him aside. "He knows something. Did you see the look on his face when I showed him that picture?"

Ronny nodded. "Yeah. But would you look at this! I got something all over my jacket. What a clod I am."

Marcus touched the spot. It smeared. "It's still wet. You must have brushed against something at the car wash." He sniffed it. "Paint!" he said. "Now what would a car wash be doing with paint?"

Ronny blotted the spot. "I was going to say painting the walls, but this is enamel." Marcus' walkie-talkie crackled. "Breaker to the Wild Goose. Breaker to the Wild Goose." It was Beth.

"You've got the Wild Goose," Marcus answered. "Go ahead."

"I just remembered something," Beth said breathlessly. "That boy had splatters of paint on his pants—several different colors. I'm sorry, but I just remembered it."

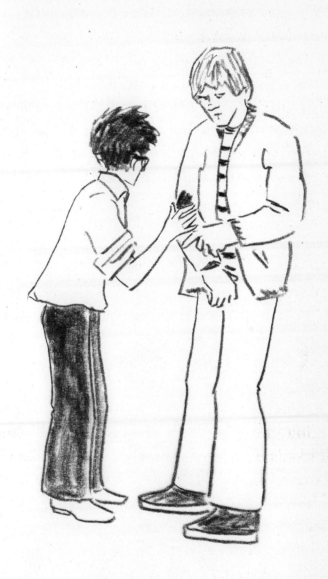

Marcus whooped. "That's a big ten four, Mother Goose. All Geese, I hope you have your ears on. I think I've got the solution!"

The walkie-talkie crackled again. "This is Goose Quill," Pete interrupted. "I'm at Main and Pine. And I see a boy that sure looks like this picture. He's eastbound on a tomato red ten speed. I'm going to follow on my wheels."

"Ten four, Goose Quill," Marcus said. "Move with caution. Geese? Did you read that last copy? Ronny and I are at Walker and Main. Eyeball here double time."

All the gang answered "ten four" for yes. In a few minutes all but Pete were gathered across from Sam's Car Wash. They stood in the alley where they couldn't be seen. But they had a good view of the car wash.

"Look!" Beth whispered. "That's him. And there's Pete behind him."

"Wow!" Tubby said. "He sure looks like the picture you drew, Ronny."

"Not really," said Ronny. "It doesn't look anything like him to me."

"Breaker to the Geese," said Pete. He was talking very softly. "I'm going to eyeball that car wash. If I give you a shout, you call the police, hear?"

"Ten four, Goose Quill," said Marcus. "Be careful."

24

The gang watched as the suspect rode the tomato red ten speed into the car wash. Pete rode by the entrance, then disappeared around the corner of the building. Minutes seemed like hours. Then Pete's voice whispered over the box, "Get the Mounties, and quick. They're on to something. They're packing up everything in a blue van. Hurry!"

Beth scrambled for the phone booth at the corner. "I told them not to advertise," she said with a wink when she returned.

Tubby stared at her blankly. "That's one I don't know."

Don said, "That means they should come without sirens and flashing lights." Tubby nodded.

In a few moments the gang and Ronny lined up on the sidewalk to watch as the police led the thieves from the car wash. Ronny sighed. "You kids are really something else. If I had your brains, I'd have never left school!"

Beth stood facing Ronny with her hands on her hips. "Honestly, Ronny! I'm getting angry now. Stop putting yourself down." Ronny started to argue but gave up when Beth continued, "Tubby is just great at math. I'm just average with it. Marcus is really smart about fixing things. Pete is good with words. None of us do everything great. We just use what we have."

Tubby nodded. "That's right, Ronny. You know a talent is something you have to take care of like a living thing, or it dies!"

Ronny scratched his chin. "Thanks anyway, gang. But it's too late for me. I'd never catch up now, even if I wanted to."

Beth waved the picture Ronny had drawn. "It looked just like him! Ronny, this is a real talent! Tubby is right. Use it, or it'll die!"

Ronny threw his hands up. "What do you want me to do? Go back where everybody is younger than I am? I'd feel stupid going to school. And who says I would do better this time?"

Don pushed his baseball cap back on his head

and wiped his brow. "Listen, Ronny. A guy came to our school. He talked about special schools where you learn a trade. He even told us about how people can do things like sign painting and cartooning and ads in the paper and stuff like that."

"I can't afford that," Ronny argued. "Why do you think I work as a delivery boy? For fun?"

"That's the best part," Pete said. "It's part of the public school system here. You don't pay. It's called 'drop in school.'"

Ronny laughed. "Oh, I get it. Drop out, drop in, huh?"

The gang nodded. "You'll do it?" Beth urged.

"I don't think so. But I promise, I'll think about it."

Several days passed and all the gang had their bikes back. Tubby's was a multi-colored green and orange monster, because the thieves hadn't finished painting it before they were caught.

"At least I don't have any trouble spotting my bike in a crowd," Tubby said while they were waiting for Marcus. The walkie-talkie crackled. "Breaker to the Geese," Marcus called.

Pete pushed the button. "You've got the Geese," he said. "Go ahead." The others leaned forward to listen.

"Got some good news and some bad news," Marcus said. "The bad news is the police never did find Ronny's bike.

"But the good news is: He doesn't really need it now. He enrolled in the trade school. He starts today."

"Great!" Mother Goose said. "What made him change his mind?"

Marcus laughed. "Oh, he said he thought about what you said. He really enjoyed drawing that day and found he missed it. And one other thing. He said he just couldn't face a flock of angry Geese!"

"That's a big ten four!" they shouted together.